The Jesuits' Church in G

By

E. T. A. Hoffmann

British Library Cataloguing-in-Publication Data
A catalogue record for this book is available from the
British Library

E. T. A. Hoffman

Ernst Theodor Wilhelm Hoffmann was born in Königsberg, East Prussia in 1776. His family were all jurists, and during his youth he was initially encouraged to pursue a career in law. However, in his late teens Hoffman became increasingly interested in literature and philosophy, and spent much of his time reading German classicists and attending lectures by, amongst others, Immanuel Kant.

In was in his twenties, upon moving with his uncle to Berlin, that Hoffman first began to promote himself as a composer, writing an operetta called Die Maske and entering a number of playwriting competitions. Hoffman struggled to establish himself anywhere for a while, flitting between a number of cities and dodging the attentions of Napoleon's occupying troops. In 1808, while living in Bamberg, he began his job as a theatre manager and a music critic, and Hoffman's break came a year later, with the publication of Ritter Gluck. The story centred on a man who meets, or thinks he has met, a long-dead composer, and played into the 'doppelgänger' theme – at that time very popular in literature. It was shortly after this that Hoffman began to use the pseudonym E. T. A. Hoffmann, declaring the 'A' to stand for 'Amadeus', as a tribute to the great composer, Mozart.

Over the next decade, while moving between Dresden, Leipzig and Berlin, Hoffman produced a great range of both literary and musical works. Probably Hoffman's most well-known story, produced in 1816, is 'The Nutcracker and the Mouse King', due to the fact that – some seventy-six years later - it inspired Tchaikovsky's ballet The Nutcracker.

In the same vein, his story 'The Sandman' provided both the inspiration for Léo Delibes's ballet Coppélia, and the basis for a highly influential essay by Sigmund Freud, called 'The Uncanny'. (Indeed, Freud referred to Hoffman as the "unrivalled master of the uncanny in literature.")

Alcohol abuse and syphilis eventually took a great toll on Hoffman though, and – having spent the last year of his life paralysed – he died in Berlin in 1822, aged just 46. His legacy is a powerful one, however: He is seen as a pioneer of both Romanticism and fantasy literature, and his novella, Mademoiselle de Scudéri: A Tale from the Times of Louis XIV is often cited as the first ever detective story.

The Jesuits' Church in G----

Packed up in a wretched post-chaise, which the moths had left from instinct--as the rats left Prospero's vessel--I at last, after a break-neck journey, stopped half dislocated, at the inn in the G---- market-place. All the possible misfortune that might have befallen me had lighted on my carriage, which lay, shattered, with the postmaster at the last stage. Four skinny, jaded horses, after a lapse of many hours, dragged up the crazy vehicle, with the help of several peasants and my own servant; knowing folks came up, shook their heads, and thought that a thorough repair, which might occupy two, or even three days would be necessary. The place seemed to me agreeable, the country pretty, and yet I felt not a little horror-struck at the delay with which I was threatened. If, gentle reader, you were ever compelled to stop three days in a little town, where you did not know a soul, but were forced to remain a stranger to every body, and if some deep pain did not destroy the inclination for social converse, you will be able to appreciate my annoyance. In words alone does the spirit of life manifest itself in all around us; but the inhabitants of your small towns are like a secluded orchestra, which has worked into its own way of playing and singing by hard practice, so that the tone of the foreigner is discordant to their ears, and at once puts them to silence. I was walking up and down my room, in a thorough ill-humour, when it at once struck me that a friend at home, who had once passed two years at G----, had often spoken of a learned, clever man, with whom he had been intimate. His name, I recollected, was Aloysius Walter, professor at the Jesuits' college. I now resolved to set out, and turn my friend's acquaintance to my own advantage. They told me at the college that Professor Walter was lecturing, but would soon have finished, and as they gave me the choice of calling again or waiting in the outer rooms, I chose the latter. The cloisters, colleges, and churches of the Jesuits are everywhere built in that Italian style which, based upon the antique form and manner, prefers splendour and elegance to holy solemnity and religious dignity. In this case the lofty, light, airy halls were adorned with rich architecture and the images of saints, which were here placed against the walls, between Ionic pillars, were singularly contrasted by the carving over the doorways, which invariably represented a dance of genii, or fruit and the dainties of the kitchen.

The professor entered--I reminded him of my friend, and claimed his hospitality for the period of my forced sojourn in the place. I found him just as my friend had described him; clear in his discourse, acquainted with the world, in short, quite in the style of the higher class priest, who has been scientifically educated, and peeping over his breviary into life, has often sought to know what is going on there. When I found his room furnished with modern elegance, I returned to my former reflections in the halls, and uttered them to the professor aloud.

"You are right," said he, "we have banished from our edifices that gloomy solemnity, that strange majesty of the crushing tyrant, who oppresses our bosoms in Gothic architecture, and causes a certain unpleasant sensation, and we have very properly endowed our works with the lively cheerfulness of the ancients."

"But," said I, "does not that sacred dignity, that lofty majesty of Gothic architecture which seems, as it were, striving after Heaven, proceed from the true spirit of Christianity, which, supersensual itself, is directly opposed to that sensual spirit of the antique world which remains in the circle of the earthly?"

The professor smiled: "The higher kingdom," said he, "should be recognised in this world, and this recognition can be awakened by cheerful symbols, such as life--nay, the spirit which descends from that kingdom into earthly life--presents. Our home is above, but while we dwell here, our kingdom is of this world also."

"Ay," thought I, "in every thing that you have done you have indeed shown that your kingdom is of this world--nay, of this world only;" but I did not communicate my thoughts to Professor Aloysius Walter, who proceeded thus:

"What you say of the magnificence of our buildings in this place can only refer properly to the pleasant appearance of the form. Here, where we cannot afford marble, and great masters in painting will not work for us, we are--in conformity with the modern fashion--obliged to make use of substitutes. If we get as high as polished plaster we have done a great deal, and our different kinds of marble are often nothing more than the work of the painter. This is the case in our church, which, thanks to the liberality of our patrons, has been newly decorated."

I expressed a desire to see the church; the professor led me down, and when I entered the Corinthian colonnade, which formed the nave of the church, I felt the pleasing--too pleasing impression of the graceful proportions. To the left of the principal altar a lofty scaffolding had been erected, upon which a man stood, who was painting over the walls in the antique style.

"Now! how are you going on, Berthold?" cried the professor.

The painter turned round to us, but immediately proceeded with his work, saying in an indistinct, and almost inaudible voice: "Great deal of trouble--crooked, confused stuff--no rule to make use of--beasts--apes--human faces-- human faces--miserable fool that I am!"

These last words he cried aloud in a voice, that nothing but the deepest agony working in the soul could produce. I felt strangely affected;--these words, the expression of face, the glance which he had previously cast at the professor, brought before my eyes the whole struggling life of an unfortunate artist. The man could have been scarcely more than forty years old; his form, though disfigured by the unseemly, dirty costume of a painter, had something in it indescribably noble, and deep grief could only discolour his face, but could not extinguish the fire that sparkled in his black eyes. I asked the professor for particulars respecting this painter: "He is a foreign artist," was the reply, "who came here just at the time when the repair of the church had been resolved upon. He undertook the work we offered him with pleasure, and indeed his arrival was for us a stroke of good fortune, since neither here, nor for a great distance round, could we find a painter so admirably fitted for all that we require. Besides, he is the most good-natured creature in the world, and we all love him heartily; for that reason he got on well in our college. Beside giving him a considerable salary for his work, we board him, which, by the way, does not entail a very heavy burden upon us, for he is abstemious almost to excess, though perhaps it may accord with the weakness of his constitution.

"But," said I, "he seemed to-day so peevish--so irritable."

"That," replied the professor, "is owing to a particular cause. But let us look at some fine pictures on the side altars, which by a lucky chance we obtained some time ago. There is only a single original--a Dominichino--among them, the rest are by unknown masters of the Italian school; but if you are free from prejudice, you will be forced to confess that every one of them might bear the most celebrated name."

I found it was exactly as the professor had said. Strangely enough, the only original was one of the weakest--if not the very, weakest of the collection, while the beauty of many of the anonymous pictures had for me an irresistible charm. The picture on one of the altars was covered up, and I asked the cause of this: "This picture," said the professor, "is the finest that we possess,--it is the work of a young artist of modern times--certainly his last, for his flight is checked. At this time we are obliged, for certain reasons, to cover it up, but to-morrow, or the day after, I shall perhaps be in a condition to show it you."

I wished to make further inquiries, but the professor hurried swiftly through the passage, and that was enough to show his unwillingness to answer more. We went back to the college, and I readily accepted the invitation of the professor, who wished me, in the afternoon, to go with him to some public gardens in the neighbourhood. We returned home late, a storm had risen, and I had scarcely reached my dwelling than the rain began to pour down. About midnight the sky cleared up, and the thunder only murmured in the distance. Through the open windows the warm air, laden with scents, entered the room, and though I was weary I could not resist the temptation to take a walk. I succeeded in waking the surly man-servant, who had been snoring for about two hours; and in showing him that there was no madness in walking at midnight. Soon I found myself in the street. When I passed the Jesuits' church, I was struck by the dazzling light that beamed through a window. The little side-door was ajar, so I entered and saw a wax-taper burning before a niche. When I had come nearer, I observed that before this niche a pack-thread net had been spread, behind which a dark form was running up and down the ladder, and seemed to be designing something on the niche. It was Berthold, who was accurately tracing the shadow of the net with black colour. On a tall easel, by the ladder, stood the drawing of an altar. I was much struck at the ingenious contrivance. If, gentle reader, you are in the least acquainted with the noble art of painting, you will once know, without further explanation, the use of the net, the shadow of which Berthold was sketching. Berthold was about to paint a projecting altar on the niche, and that he might make a large copy of the small drawing with due correctness, he was obliged to put a net, in the usual manner, over both the sketch and the surface on which the sketch was to be completed. In this instance he had to paint not on a flat surface but on a semicircular one; and the correspondence of the squares which the curved lines of the net formed on the concave surface, with the straight ones of the sketch, together with accuracy in the architectural proportions which were to be brought forward in perspective, could not be otherwise obtained than by that simple and ingenious contrivance. I was cautious enough not to step before the taper, lest I might betray myself by my shadow, but I stood near enough to his side to observe the painter closely. He appeared to me quite another man. Perhaps it was the effect of the taper, but his face had a good colour, his eyes sparkled with internal satisfaction, and when he had completed the lines he placed himself before the screen, with his hands resting on his sides, and looking at his work, whistled a merry tune. He now turned round, and tore down the net. Suddenly he was struck by my figure, and cried aloud:

"Halloah! halloah! is that you, Christian?"

I went up to him, explained how I had been attracted into the church, and praising the ingenious contrivance of the net, gave him to understand that I was but a connoisseur and practiser of the noble art of painting. Without making me any further answer, Berthold said:

"Christian is neither more nor less than a sluggard. He was to have kept with me faithfully through the whole night, and now he is certainly snoring somewhere! I must get on with my work, for probably it will be bad to paint here on the screen to-morrow--and yet I can do nothing by myself."

I offered my assistance, upon which he laughed aloud, laid hold of both my shoulders, and cried:

"That is a capital joke! What will Christian say, when he finds to-morrow that he is an ass, and that I have done without him? So, come hither, stranger, help me to build a little."

He lit several tapers, we ran through the church, pulled together a number of blocks and planks, and a lofty scaffold was soon raised within the screen.

"Now hand up quickly," cried Berthold, as he ascended.

I was astonished at the rapidity with which Berthold made a large copy of the drawing; he drew his lines boldly, and always clearly and correctly, without a single fault. Having been accustomed to such matters in my early youth, I was of good service to him, for standing, now above him, now below him, I fixed the long rulers at the points he indicated, and held them fast, pointed the charcoal, and handed it to him, and so on.

"You are a capital assistant," cried Berthold, quite delighted.

"And you," I retorted, "are one of the best architectural

painters possible. But tell me, have you applied your bold, ready hand to no sort of painting but this?--Pardon the question."

"What do you mean?" said Berthold.

"Why, I mean," replied I, "that you are fit for something better than painting church walls with marble pillars. Architectural painting is, after all, something subordinate; the historical painter, the landscape painter, stands infinitely higher. With them, mind and fancy, no longer confined to the narrow limits of geometrical lines, take a higher flight. Even the only fantastic part of your painting, that perspective, which deceives the senses, depends upon accurate calculation, and the result therefore is the product not of genius, but of mathematical speculation." While I was speaking thus, the painter laid aside his pencil, and rested his head on his hand.

"Friend stranger," he began, in a solemn, indistinct voice, "thou speakest profanely, when thou endeavourest to arrange the different branches of art according to rank, like the vassals of some proud king. And still more profane is it, when thou only esteemest those presumptuous fools who, being deaf to the clang of the fetters that enslave them, and being without feeling for the pressure of the earthy, wish to think themselves free--yea, even to be gods--and to rule light and life after their own fashion. Dost thou know the fable of Prometheus, who wished to be a creator, and stole fire from heaven to animate his lifeless figures? He succeeded; the forms stalked living along, and from their eyes beamed forth that heavenly fire that burned within them; but the

15

impious being, who had dared to attempt the divine, was condemned to fearful, endless torment, without redemption. The heart which had felt the divine, in which the desire after the unearthly had awakened, was torn by the vulture, to which revenge had given birth, and which now fed upon the vitals of the presumptuous one. He who has attempted the heavenly, feels earthly pain for ever."

The painter stood absorbed in his own reflections.

"Berthold," I exclaimed, "what has all this to do with your art? I do not think that any one can deem it presumption to present the human form, either by painting or sculpture."

"Um, ha," laughed Berthold, in wild derision; "child's play is no presumption. It is all child's play with those folks, who comfortably dip their pencils into colour-pots, and daub a canvass with the veritable desire of producing human beings; but it always turns out as if some drudge of nature had undertaken to make men, as it stands in that tragedy, and had failed. Such as those are no presumptuous sinners, but poor innocent fools. But if one strives to attain the highest, not the mere sensual, like Titian--no, the highest in divine nature, the Promethean spark in man--that is a precipice--a narrow edge on which we stand--the abyss is open! The bold sailor soars above him, and a devilish deceit lets him perceive that below, which he wished to see above the stars." The painter uttered a deep sigh, passed his hand over his forehead, and then looked upwards. "But why do I talk all this mad stuff to you, comrade, and leave off painting? Look here, mate, this is what I call well and honestly drawn. How noble is the rule!

All the lines combine to a determined end--a determined, clearly conceived effect. Only that which is done by measure is purely human;--what is beyond, is of evil. Can we not conceive that the Deity has expressly created us, to manage for his own good purpose that which is exhibited according to measured, appreciable rules;--in a word, the purely commeasurable, just as we, in our turn build saw-mills and spinning-machines, as the mechanical superintendents of our wants? Professor Walter lately maintained, that certain beasts were merely created to be eaten by others, and that this in the end, conduced to our own utility. Thus, for example, cats, he said, had an innate propensity to devour mice, that they might not nibble the sugar placed ready for our breakfast. And the professor was right in the end;--animals, and we ourselves are but well-ordered machines, made to work up and knead certain materials for the table of the unknown king.--Come, come, mate, hand me up the pots. I prepared all the tones yesterday by daylight, that this candlelight might not deceive us, and they all stand numbered in yonder corner. Hand me up No. 1, young friend. Gray with gray!--What would dry, weary life be, if the Lord of Heaven had not put so many motley playthings into our hands. He who demeans himself well does not, like the curious boy, try to break the box from which the music comes when he turns the handle. It is just natural, they say, that it sounds inside, for I turn the handle. Because I have drawn this intellective correctly according to the point of view, I know that it will have the effect of actual sculpture on the spectator.--Now, boy, reach me No. 2, now

I paint in colours that are toned down according to rule, and it appears receding five yards. All that I know well enough--oh, we are amazingly clever! How is it that objects diminish in the distance? This one stupid question of a Chinese could put to confusion Professor Eytelwein himself; but he could help himself out with the music-box, and say he had often turned the handle, and always experienced the same result.--Violet, No. 2, youngster! Another rule, and a thick washed-out brush! Ah, what is all our striving and struggling after the higher, but the helpless, unconscious act of an infant who hurts the nurse that feeds him. Violet, No. 2! Quick, young man! The ideal is an evil, lying dream, produced by fermented blood. Take away the pot, young man, I am coming down. The devil lures us with puppets, to which he glues angel's wings."

I am unable to repeat literally, what Berthold said, while he went on painting rapidly, and treated me only as his fag. He went on in the tone in which he had begun, scoffing at the limited nature of every human effort. Ah, I was inspecting the depth of a mind that had received its death-wound, and that only uttered its complaints in bitter irony. Morning dawned, and the glimmer of the taper grew pale before the entrance of sunlight. Berthold painted on zealously, but he became more and more silent, and only single sounds--ultimately, only sighs--escaped his burdened breast. He had planned the entire altar with all its gradation of colour, and even now the picture stood out quite prominently.

"Admirable! admirable!" I cried out with delight.

"Do you think," said Berthold, faintly, "that I shall make something of it? I at least took great pains to make my drawing correct, but now I can do no more."

"No, no, not a stroke more, dear Berthold," I exclaimed, "it is almost incredible how you have made so much progress in such a work within a few hours. But you exert yourself too much, and are quite lavish of your power."

"And yet," said Berthold, "these are my happiest hours. Perhaps I talked too much, but it is only in words that the pain which consumes my vitals finds a vent."

"You seem to feel very unhappy, my poor friend," said I, "some frightful event has had an evil influence on your life."

The painter slowly took his materials into the chapel, extinguished the lights, and coming up to me, seized my hand, and said, in a faltering voice, "Could you be cheerful, nay, could you have one quiet moment, if you were conscious of a fearful, irreparable crime?"

I stood perfectly amazed. The bright sunbeams fell on the painter's pallid, agitated countenance, and he almost looked like a spectre as he staggered through the little door into the interior of the college.

I could scarcely wait for the hour on the following day, when Professor Walter had appointed to see me. I told him the whole affair of the previous night, which had excited me not a little; I described in the most lively colours the strange conduct of the painter, and did not suppress a word that he had uttered--not even those, which related to himself. But the more I hoped for the professor's sympathy, the more indifferent he appeared; nay, he smiled upon me in a most unpleasant manner when I continued to talk of Berthold, and pressed him to tell me all he knew about this unfortunate man.

"He is a strange creature that painter," said the professor, "mild, good-tempered, sober, industrious, as I told you before, but weak in his intellect. If he had been otherwise he would never have descended, even though he did commit a crime, from a great historical painter, to a poor dauber of walls."

This expression, "dauber of walls," annoyed me as much as the professor's general indifference. I tried to convince him that Berthold was even now a most estimable artist, and deserving of the highest, the most active sympathy.

"Well," said the professor at last, "since you take so much interest in Berthold you shall hear all that I know of him, and that is not a little. By way of introduction we will go into the church at once. As Berthold has worked hard throughout the night he will rest during the forenoon. If we found him in the church my design would fail."

We went to the church, the professor had the cloth removed from the covered picture, and a work of the most magical splendour, such as I had never seen, was revealed to me. The composition was in the style of Raffaelle, simple and of heavenly sublimity. Mary and Elizabeth were sitting on the grass in a beautiful garden; the children, Jesus and John, were before them, playing with flowers, and in the background towards the side, a male figure was praying. Mary's lovely, heavenly face, the dignity and elevation of her entire figure, filled me with astonishment and the deepest admiration. She was beautiful, more beautiful than an earthly woman, and her glance indicated the higher power of the mother of God, like that of Raffaelle's Mary in the Dresden Gallery. Ah! was not the deepest thirst for eternity awakened perforce in the human heart, by those wondrous eyes round which a deep shadow was floating? Did not those soft, half-opened lips speak in consolatory language, as in the sweet melody of angels, of the infinite happiness of heaven? An indescribable feeling impelled me to cast myself down in the dust before her, the Queen of Heaven. I had lost the power of speech, and could not turn my eyes from the incomparable figure. Only Mary and the children were quite finished; the last touch had not, apparently, been given to the figure of Elizabeth, and the praying man was not yet painted over. Approaching nearer, I perceived in this man the features of Berthold, and already anticipated in my mind what the professor presently said: "This picture is Berthold's last work. We got it several years ago from N----, in Upper Silesia, where one of our colleagues bought it at an auction. Although unfinished, we had it fitted in here, in the place of the wretched altar-piece which we had formerly. When Berthold first came and saw the picture, he uttered a loud shriek and fell senseless to the ground. Afterwards he carefully avoided looking at it, and told me in confidence that it was his last work of this class. I hoped that I should gradually persuade him to finish it, but every proposal of the sort he rejected with the utmost abhorrence, and to keep him in good spirits, and in the full possession of his powers, I was forced to cover up the picture so long as he remained in the church. If it met his eye only by accident, he ran as if impelled by some irresistible power, cast himself sobbing on the ground, a paroxysm seized him, and he was for many days quite unfit for work."

"Poor unfortunate man!" exclaimed I, "how did the hand of the devil take such a deadly hold of thy life?"

"Oh!" cried the professor, "the hand as well as the arm grew in his own body: he was his own demon, his own Lucifer, flashing the infernal torch upon his own life. That is plain enough to those who know his biography."

I entreated the professor at once to tell me all that he knew about the life of the unfortunate painter.

"That would be much too prolix, and cost too much breath," replied the professor. "Do not let us spoil the cheerful day by such gloomy stuff. We will take breakfast and then go to the mill, where an excellent dinner awaits us."

I did not desist from my requests to the professor, and after much talk on both sides, it came out that, immediately after Berthold's arrival, a youth who was studying at the college, devotedly attached himself to him, and that Berthold, by degrees, communicated the particulars of his life to this youth, who had carefully written them down, and had given the manuscript to the professor.

"He was," said the professor, "much such an enthusiast as--pardon me--you are! But this work of writing down the strange events in the painter's life served him as a capital exercise for style."

With much trouble I obtained from the professor a promise that he would lend me the manuscript after the close of our pleasure-party. Whether it proceeded from my own violent curiosity, or whether it was the professor's fault, I never felt more uneasy than during this day. The icy coldness of the professor when speaking of Berthold had been repulsive to me, but his conversation with his colleagues who participated in the repast, convinced me, that in spite of all his learning, and all his knowledge of the world, he had no sense for the sublime, and was as gross a materialist as possible. The system of consuming and being consumed, as Berthold called it, he had actually adopted. All mental endeavours, all the powers of creation and invention, he deduced from certain states of the stomach and the entrails, uttering on this subject all sorts of monstrous conceits. Thus, for instance, he very seriously maintained that every thought proceeded from the marriage of two fibres in the human brain. I perceived how the professor, with all this absurd stuff, must torment poor Berthold, who, in the irony of despair, attacked the notion of any favourable influence from a higher region, and how he must plunge pointed daggers into wounds still fresh and bleeding. The evening at last came, and the professor put a few sheets of manuscript into my hand, with the words: "There, my dear enthusiast, is the student's handy work. It is not badly written but very odd, and the author, against all rule, thrusts in discourses of the painter, word for word, without any notice to the reader. I will make you a present of the work, of which I have a right to dispose by virtue of my office, for I know perfectly well that you are no writer. The author of the "Fantasie-Stuecke in Callot's Manier,"[1] (fancy pieces in the style of Callot) would have cut it according to his own mad fashion, and would have printed it at once. I have nothing of the sort to expect from you."

Professor Aloysius Walter did not know that he really stood before the "travelling enthusiast," although he might have found it out, and thus, gentle reader, I am enabled to give you the Jesuit-student's short history of the painter, Berthold. It thoroughly explains the manner in which he conducted himself in my presence, and thou, reader, wilt be able to see how the strange spirit of destiny often plunges us into destructive error.

* * * * *

"'Only let your son make up his mind and go to Italy. He is already a clever artist, and here at D---- there is no lack of opportunity for studying after excellent originals in every class, but here he must not stay. The free life of an artist must dawn upon him in the cheerful land of art, his studies will there first take a living form, and produce individual thoughts. Mere copying is now of no further use to him. The growing plant requires more sun to thrive and bring forth its blossoms and fruit. Your son has a really artistical temperament, so you may be perfectly satisfied about all the rest!' Thus said the old painter, Stephan Birkner, to Berthold's parents. The latter scraped together all that their slender means would allow to fit out the youth for his long journey, and thus was Berthold's warmest wish--that of travelling to Italy--accomplished.

"When Birkner told me the decision of my parents, I literally jumped for joy. I wandered about as in a dream till the time of my departure. I was not able to make a single stroke with my pencil in the gallery. I made the inspector, and all the artists who had been to Italy, tell me of the land where art flourishes. The day and hour at length arrived. The parting from my parents was painful, as they felt a gloomy presentiment that they should not see me again. Even my father, generally a firm, resolute man, had difficulty in containing his feelings. 'Italy! you will see Italy!' cried my brother artists, and then my wish shone forth with greater power, from my deep melancholy, and I stepped boldly forth, for the path of an artist seemed to begin even at my parents' door.'

"Berthold had studied every department of painting, but he had especially devoted himself to landscapes, at which he worked with ardent love and zeal. In Rome he expected to find abundant nurture for this branch of art, but it proved otherwise. The very circle of artists and dilettanti in which he moved, continually told him that the historical painter alone stood on the highest point, and that all the rest were but subordinate. He was advised, if he wished to become an artist of eminence, to abandon at once the department he had chosen, and to devote himself to the higher branch; and this advice, coupled with the novel impression which Raffaelle's mighty frescoes in the Vatican had made upon him, determined him to give up landscape painting altogether. He sketched after the Raffaelles, and he copied small oil paintings by other celebrated masters. All these things were very cleverly done by his practised hand; but he plainly felt that the praise of the artists and dilettanti should only solace him, and encourage him to further efforts. He himself saw that his sketches and copies wanted all the fire of the originals. Raffaelle's and Correggio's heavenly thoughts- -so he thought--inspired him to creations of his own, but he wished to hold them fast in his fancy, they vanished as in a mist, and all that he sketched was like every obscure, confused thought, without motion and significance. During his vain endeavours deep melancholy took possession of his soul, and he often escaped from his friends, privately to sketch and paint in the vicinity of Rome, groups of trees--single pieces of landscape. But even these attempts were less successful than formerly; and, for the first time in his life, he doubted the truth of his calling as an artist. His proudest hopes seemed on the point of vanishing. 'Ah, my revered friend and instructor,' wrote Berthold to Birkner, 'you gave me credit for great things; but here, when a light should have risen in my soul, I have learned that that which you termed real artistical genius was nothing but a sort of talent--mere dexterity of hand. Tell my parents that I shall soon return, and learn some trade that I may get my living,' &c. Birkner wrote back: 'Oh! would I could be with you, my son, to support you in your depression. It is your very doubts that prove your calling as an artist. He who with steady immoveable confidence in his powers believes that he will always progress, is a blind fool, who only deceives himself, for he wants the proper spur to endeavour, which only consists in the thought of deficiency. Persevere and you will soon gain strength; and then, no longer fettered by the opinion or the advice of friends, who are, perhaps, unable to appreciate you, you will quietly pursue the path which your own nature has designed for you. It will then be left to your own decision whether you become a painter of landscapes or historical pieces, and you will cease to think of a hostile separation of the branches of one trunk.'

"It happened that about the time when Berthold received this letter of consolation from his old friend and instructor, Philip Hackert's fame became widely extended in Rome. Some of the paintings which he had exhibited, and which were distinguished by wonderful grace and clearness, proved the real genius of the artist, and even the historical painters admitted that there was much greatness and excellence in this pure imitation of nature. Berthold breathed again; he no more heard his favourite art treated with contempt, he saw a man who pursued it honoured and elevated, and, as it were, a spark fell on his soul that he must travel to Naples and study under Hackert. In high spirits he wrote to Birkner, and his parents, that he had now, after a hard struggle, discovered the right way, and hoped to become a clever artist in his own style. The honest German, Hackert, received his German pupil with great kindness, and the latter soon made great efforts to follow his master. Berthold attained great facility in giving faithful representations of the different kinds of trees and shrubs, and was not a little successful in those misty effects, which are to be found in Hackert's pictures. He thus gained great praise, but it seemed to him as if something was wanting both in his own and his master's landscapes;--something to which he could not give a name, and which was nevertheless plainly apparent in the pictures by Claude Lorraine, and the wild landscapes of Salvator Rosa. Soon he felt a want of confidence in his instructor, and he felt particularly dispirited when Hackert, with unwearied exertion, painted some dead game which the king had sent him. Soon, however, he conquered such presumptuous thoughts--as he considered them--and went on with virtuous resignation and true German industry, following the pattern of his master, so that in a short time he could nearly equal him. At Hackert's own suggestion he sent a large landscape, which he had faithfully copied from nature, to an exhibition, which was chiefly to consist of landscapes and pieces of still-life in the Hackert style. All the artists and connoisseurs admired the young man's faithful, neatly executed works, and praised him aloud. There was only an elderly strangely-attired man who did not say a word about Hackert's pictures, but smiled, significantly, whenever the multitude broke out into extravagant praises. Berthold perceived plainly enough that this stranger, when he stood before his landscape, shook his head with an air of the deepest pity, and was then about to retire. Being somewhat elevated by the general praise which he had received, Berthold could not help feeling indignant with the stranger. He went up to him, and speaking more sharply than was necessary, said:

'You do not seem satisfied with the picture, sir, although I must say there are excellent artists and connoisseurs who do not think it so bad. Pray tell me where the fault lies that I may improve the picture according to your kind suggestion.' The stranger cast a keen glance at Berthold, and said, very seriously: 'Young man, a great deal might be made out of you.' Berthold felt deeply horrified at the glance and words of this man; he had not courage to say any thing more, or to follow him, when he slowly stalked out of the saloon. Hackert soon came in himself, and Berthold hastened to tell him of his meeting with this strange man. 'Ha!' said Hackert, smiling, 'do not take that to heart. That is a crabbed old man, who grumbles at every thing, and is pleased at nothing; I met him in the ante-room. He was born of Greek parents, in Malta, and is a rich, queer old fellow, and no bad painter. All that he does has a fantastic appearance, and this proceeds from the absurd notion he has about art, and from the fact that he has constructed a system which is utterly worthless. I know well enough that he has no opinion of me, which I readily pardon in him, since he cannot throw any doubt on my honourably acquired fame.' Berthold had felt as if the Maltese had touched a sore place in his soul, like a beneficent physician, only for the purpose of probing it and healing it; but he soon drove this notion from his mind, and worked on happily as he had done before.

"The success of this large picture, which was universally admired, gave him courage to begin a companion to it. Hackert himself selected one of the most lovely spots in

29

the gorgeous vicinity of Naples; and, as the first picture had represented sunset, this landscape was to show the effect of sunrise. He had a number of strange trees, a number of vineyards, and, above all, a good deal of mist to paint.

"Berthold was sitting on a large flat stone, in this very spot, completing the sketch of the great picture after nature. 'Bravo--well done!' said a voice near him. He looked up. The Maltese was viewing his work, and added, with a sarcastic smile, 'You have only forgotten one thing, my dear young friend. Only look yonder, at the wall of the distant vineyard; the one covered with green tendrils. The door is half-open, don't you see? You must represent that with its proper shading. The half-open door makes a surprising effect!'

"'You are joking, sir,' exclaimed Berthold, 'and without reason. Such accidental circumstances are by no means so contemptible as you imagine, and for that very reason my master loves to employ them. Only recollect the suspended white cloth in the landscape of one of the Dutch painters, that could not be omitted without marring the general effect. You, however, seem to be no friend to landscape painting in general; and, as I have given myself up to it with heart and soul, I beg of you to let me go on working in quiet.'

"'You are much mistaken, young man,' said the Maltese. 'I tell you again that a good deal might be made of you, for your works visibly prove an unwearied endeavour to attain the highest; but that, unfortunately, you will never attain, since the path that you have taken does not lead to it. Only mark what I tell you. Perhaps I may succeed in kindling that flame in your soul, which you, senseless as you are, are endeavouring to smother, and in making it flash up brightly, so as to enlighten you. Then you will be able to recognise the real spirit that animates you. Do you think I am so foolish as to place the landscape lower in rank than the historical painting, and that I do not recognise the common goal after which the painters of both classes should strive? The apprehension of nature in the deepest import of that higher sense, which kindles all beings to a higher life, that is the sacred end of all art. Can the mere dim copying of nature lead to this? How poor, how stiff and forced, is the appearance of a manuscript copied from another in some foreign language, which the copyist does not understand, and is, therefore, unable to give the strokes, which he laboriously imitates, their proper significance. Thus your master's landscapes are correct copies of an original author in a language which is strange to him. The initiated artist hears the voice of nature, which from trees, hedges, flowers, mountains, and waters, speaks to him, and of unfathomable mysteries in wondrous sounds, which form themselves in his bosom to a pious feeling of foreboding; then, as a divine spirit, the talent itself of transferring this dim feeling to his works, descends upon him. Have not you yourself, young man, felt strangely affected when looking at the landscapes of the old masters? Assuredly you did not think whether the leaves of the lime trees, the pines, the plane trees, might be truer to nature, whether the back ground might be more misty, or the water might be clearer; but the spirit that breathes from the whole raised you into a higher region, the reflection of which you seemed to behold. Therefore, study nature in the mechanical part, sedulously and carefully, that you may attain the practice of representation; but do not take the practice for the art itself. If you have penetrated into the deep import of nature, her pictures will arise within you in bright magnificence.' The Maltese was silent; but when Berthold, deeply moved by what he had heard, stood with downcast eyes, and incapable of uttering a word, the Maltese left him, saying, 'I had no intention of interrupting you in your calling, but I know that a higher spirit is slumbering in you. I called upon it, with strong words, that it might awake, and move its wings with freshness and vigour. Farewell.'

"Berthold felt as if the Maltese had only clothed in words that which had already been fermenting in his soul. The inner voice broke forth. 'No! All this striving, this constant endeavour, is but the uncertain, deceptive groping of the blind. Away with all that has hitherto dazzled me.' He was not in a condition to accomplish a single other stroke. He left his master, and wandered about full of wild uneasiness, loudly imploring that the high knowledge of which the Maltese had spoken might be revealed to him.

"'Only in sweet dreams was I happy--yes, truly blessed! Then every thing that the Maltese had spoken became true. I lay in the green hedge, while magical exhalations played around me, and the voice of nature sounded audibly and melodiously through the dark forest. 'Listen, listen, oh! thou initiated one. Hear the original tones of creation, which fashion themselves to beings accessible to thy mind.' And when I heard the chords sound plainer and plainer, I felt as though a new sense was awakened in me, and apprehended with wonderful perspicuity, that which had appeared unfathomable. As if in strange hieroglyphics I drew in the air the secrets that had been revealed to me with characters of fire; and this hieroglyphic writing was a strange landscape, upon which trees, hedges, flowers, and waters moved, as it seemed, in loud delightful sounds.'

"But it was only in dreams that poor Berthold felt real happiness, for his strength was broken, and his mind was more disturbed than it had been in Rome, when he wished to be an historical painter. If he strode through the dark wood, an unpleasant sensation of awe came over him; if he went out and looked into the distant mountains, he felt as though icy cold claws grasped his heart--his breath was stopped--and he felt as if he perished from internal anguish. All nature, which used to smile kindly upon him, became a threatening monster, and her voice, which used to greet him sweetly in the murmuring of the evening breeze, in the bubbling of the brook, in the rustling of the leaves, now told him of nothing but perdition. At last, however, the more these lively dreams consoled him, the calmer he became; nevertheless, he avoided being alone in the open air, and hence he associated himself with a couple of cheerful German painters, and took with them many a trip to the loveliest spots of Naples.

"One of them, whom we will call Florentin, was at this moment more intent upon the enjoyment of life, than upon the serious study of his art, as his portfolio sufficiently testified. Groups of dancing peasant-girls, processions, rural festivals--all this class of subjects he could transfer to paper with a sure, ready hand, whenever he chanced to meet with them. Every drawing, even though it were a mere sketch, had life and motion. At the same time his mind was by no means closed to the higher in art; on the contrary, he penetrated more than any modern painter into the strange import of the paintings by all masters. In his sketch-book he had copied in outline the frescoes of an old convent-church in Rome, before the walls were pulled down. They represented the martyrdom of St. Catharine, and one could not see any thing more beautiful, more happily conceived than those outlines, which made a very peculiar impression upon Berthold. He saw flashes through the gloomy desert that surrounded him, and the result was, that he became capable of appreciating the cheerful mind of Florentin, and that, as the latter when representing the charms, especially brought forward the human principle, he also took this principle as the ground on which he must stand, not to float away into boundless space. While Florentin was hastily sketching some group that he met, Berthold took the opportunity of looking into his book, and tried to imitate the lovely figure of Catharine, in which he was tolerably successful, although, as at Rome, he failed in giving his figures the animation of the original. He complained of this to Florentin, whom he looked upon as far his superior in true artistical genius, and at the same time told him all that the Maltese had spoken about art.

'The Maltese is right, dear brother Berthold,' said Florentin, 'and I rank the genuine landscape quite as high as the deeply significant sacred histories, as depicted by the old masters. Nay, I maintain that one ought first to strengthen oneself by the representation of that organic nature which is nearest to us, that we may be able to find light for her darker regions. I advise you, Berthold, to practise yourself in sketching figures, and in arranging your thoughts in them. Perhaps by this means you will gain additional light.' Berthold acted according to the suggestion of his friend, and it seemed to him, as if the dark clouds which spread over his life, were passing away.

"I endeavoured to represent that, which seemed no more than a mere obscure feeling in my innermost soul, by hieroglyphic characters, as I had done in my dream; but the hieroglyphics became human figures, which moved about a focus of light in strange combinations. This focus was to be the noblest form that ever was evoked by a painter's fancy, but I vainly endeavoured, when this form appeared to me in a dream, surrounded by the rays of heaven, to catch the features. Every attempt to represent it proved an utter failure, and I seemed to fade away in a state of the most ardent desire.' Florentin perceived the situation of his friend, who was excited to a morbid degree, and gave him all the consolation in his power. Often did he tell him that this was the very time when illumination would break upon him; but Berthold merely slunk about like a dreamer, and all his attempts were but the feeble efforts of a puny child.

"In the vicinity of Naples was a duke's villa from which there was the finest view of Vesuvius and the sea, and which, on this account was hospitably kept open for foreign artists, especially landscape painters. Berthold had often worked here, but still oftener in a grotto in the park had he given himself up to his fantastic dreams. One day he was sitting in this grotto tortured by the sense of longing, that tore his bosom, and was shedding briny tears, hoping that the star would shine upon his obscure path, when a rustling was heard in the hedges, and the form of an exquisitely beautiful woman was before him.

"'The sunbeams fell upon her angelic countenance: she cast upon me an indescribable glance. It was Saint Catharine. No, more than she, it was my ideal. Mad with transport I threw myself on the ground, and the form vanished with a benignant smile! My most ardent prayer was realised.'

"Florentin entered the grotto, and was surprised at Berthold, who, with beaming countenance, pressed him to his heart, while the tears streamed from his eyes. 'My friend! my friend!' he stammered forth; 'I am happy--I am blessed-- she is found--found!' He hurried to his atelier, and stretching the canvass began to paint as if inspired by divine power, he charmed before him the superterrestrial woman--for so he thought her--with the full glow of life. From this moment his inmost soul was entirely changed. Far from feeling that melancholy which preyed upon his heart, he was serene and cheerful. He industriously studied the chefs-d'oeuvre of the old painters. Many of his copies were perfectly successful, and now, for the first time, he began to produce paintings which caused astonishment among all the connoisseurs. As for landscapes, they were no more to be thought of, and Hackert himself confessed that the youth had not till now discovered his proper vocation. He had to paint many large works, such as altar-pieces for churches, and generally selected the more cheerful subjects of Christian tradition. From all of these, however, the noble form of his ideal beamed forth. It was discovered that the face and figure of the Princess Angiola T---- were represented to the life; nay, this fact was communicated to the young painter himself, and knowing folks waggishly insinuated that the German was smitten to the heart by the brilliant eyes of the lovely dame. Berthold was highly indignant at this silly gossip of people who wished to lower the heavenly into the mere earthy. 'Do you believe,' he said, 'that such a being could wander here upon earth? No; the highest was revealed in a wondrous vision; it was the moment when the artist receives consecration.' Berthold lived happy, until the French army, after Bonaparte's conquests in Italy, approached the kingdom of Naples, and the revolution, which so fearfully destroyed all the peaceful relations of the place, broke out. The king and queen had left Naples, and the Citta was appointed. The vicar-general concluded a disgraceful truce with the French commander, and the French commissaries soon came to receive the sums that were to be paid them. The vicar-general fled to escape the rage of the people, who believed themselves deserted by him, by the Citta, and, in short, by all who could defend them against the approaching enemy. Then were all the bands of society loosened. The people, in a state of wild anarchy, set law and order at defiance, and with the cry, 'Viva la Santa Fede!' wild hordes ran through the streets plundering and burning the houses of the nobles, who they thought had sold them to the enemy. Vain were the endeavours of Moliterno and Rocca Romana, who were the favourites of the people, and had been elected for leaders: vain were their endeavours to restore order. The dukes Delia Torre and Clement Filomarino were murdered, but the thirst for blood among the raging people was not yet satisfied. Berthold had just been able to escape, half-dressed, from a burning house, when he met a mob, that with kindled torches and glittering knives, was hurrying to the palace of the Duke of T----. These madmen, taking him for one of their own class, carried him along with them, shouting, 'Viva la Santa Fede!' and in a few minutes the duke, the servants, every one who resisted, were murdered, and the palace, into which Berthold was more and more forced by the throng, was in flames. Thick clouds of smoke rolled through the long passages. Berthold, in danger of being burned to death, darted through the now open doors in hopes of finding an outlet, but all in vain; a piercing shriek of agony struck his ear, and he rushed into the hall. A woman was struggling with a lazzarone, who held her fast, and was about to plunge a knife in her heart. It was the princess--it was Berthold's ideal! Losing all consciousness with horror, he sprang towards them, and it was but the work of a moment to seize the lazzarone, to fling him to the ground, to plunge his own knife in his throat, to catch the princess in his arms, to fly with her through the flaming ruins, to dash down the steps, and to go on-- on--through the dense crowd of people. None attempted to stop him in his flight. With the bloody knife in his hand, with his face begrimed by smoke, with his clothes torn, he was taken for a plunderer and murderer by the people, who willingly conceded him his prey. In a deserted corner of the city, beneath an old wall, to which, as if by instinct he had run to escape danger, he fell exhausted. On recovering, he found the princess kneeling at his side, and washing his forehead with cold water. 'Oh thanks!--thanks!' said she, in the softest and most lovely voice; 'thanks to the saints that thou hast recovered, my preserver, my all!' Berthold raised himself,--he fancied he was dreaming, he looked with fixed eyes upon the princess--yes, it was herself--the celestial form which had kindled the divine spark in his breast. 'Is it possible?--Is it true?--Do I live?' he exclaimed. 'Yes,' replied the princess, 'thou livest for me. That which thou didst not venture even to hope, has happened through a miracle. Oh! I know thee well,--thou art the German painter, Berthold, who loved me, and ennobled me in his beautiful works. Was it then possible for me to be thine? But now I am thine for ever--let us fly!' A strange feeling, as when a sudden pain disturbs sweet dreams, darted through Berthold as the princess spoke. But when the lovely woman clasped him with her full, snow-white arms, when he pressed her passionately to his bosom, then did a delicious trembling, hitherto unknown, take possession of him, and in the mad delight of possessing the greatest earthly felicity, he cried: 'Oh, it was no delirious dream! No! it is my wife whom I embrace, and whom I will never leave!'

"Escape from the city was at first impossible, for at the gate stood the French army, whose entrance the people, although badly armed and without leaders, were able to dispute for two days. Berthold, however, succeeded in flying with Angiola from one hiding-place to another, and at last out of the city. Angiola, deeply enamoured of him, could not think of remaining in Italy; she wished her family to consider her dead, that Berthold's possession of her might be secure. A diamond necklace, and some valuable rings which she wore, were sufficient to provide them with all necessaries at Rome--whither they had proceeded by slow degrees--and they arrived happily at M----, in Southern Germany, where Berthold intended to settle, and to support himself by his art. Was it not a state of felicity, not even to be dreamed, that Angiola, that creature of celestial loveliness, that ideal of his most delightful visions, now became his own,--when all social laws had seemed to raise an insurmountable barrier between him and his beloved? Berthold could hardly comprehend his happiness, he was abandoned to inexpressible delight, until the inner voice became louder and louder, urging him to think of his art. He determined to found his fame at M---- by a large picture which he designed for the Maria church there. The whole subject was to be the very simple one of Mary and Elizabeth sitting on the grass in a beautiful garden, with the infant Christ and John playing before them;

but all his efforts to obtain a pure spiritual view of his picture proved fruitless. As in that unhappy period of the crisis the forms floated away from him, and it was not the heavenly Mary--no, it was an earthly woman, his Angiola herself, fearfully distorted, that stood before the eyes of his mind. He fancied that he could defy the gloomy power that seemed to grasp him,--he prepared his colours and began to paint; but his strength was broken, and all his endeavours were--as they had been formerly--only the puny efforts of a senseless child. Whatever he painted was stiff and inanimate, and even Angiola,--Angiola his ideal, became, when she sat to him, and he tried to paint her, a mere wax image on the canvass, staring at him with its glassy eyes. His soul became more and more the prey of a despondency, that consumed all the happiness of his life. He would not, nay, he could not, work any more; and thus he fell into a state of poverty, which was the more crushing, because Angiola did not utter a word of complaint.

"'The grief that gnawed more and more into my soul, that grief that was the offspring of a hope, invariably deceived, when I summoned powers that were no longer mine, soon reduced me to a state that might be compared to madness. My wife bore me a son,--that increased my misery, and my long suppressed discontent broke out into open, burning hate. She--she alone had been the cause of my unhappiness. She was not the ideal which had appeared to me, but had only assumed the form and face of that heavenly woman. In wild despair I cursed her and her innocent child. I wished them both dead, that I might be freed from the insupportable pains that tortured me, like so many burning knives. Thoughts of hell arose in my mind. In vain did I read in Angiola's corpse-like face, and in her tears, the madness and impiety of my conduct. 'Thou hast cheated me out of my life, cursed woman!' I thundered forth, and thrust her away with my foot, when she fell fainting to the ground and clasped my knees.'

"Berthold's mad, cruel conduct towards his wife and child excited the attention of the neighbours, who informed the magistrates of the circumstance. They wished to imprison him; but when the police entered his dwelling, he had vanished with his wife and child, without leaving so much as a trace behind. Soon afterwards he appeared at N----, in Upper Silesia; he had got rid of his wife and child, and cheerfully began to paint the picture which he had vainly attempted at M----. However he could only finish the Virgin Mary, and the children--Christ and John--for he fell into a dreadful illness, which brought him near the death he desired. Every thing that belonged to him, including the unfinished picture, was sold for his subsistence; and, after he had recovered, in some measure, he departed, a sick, miserable beggar. He afterwards gained a poor livelihood by a few jobs of wall-painting."

* * * * *

"There is something terrible in the history of Berthold," said I to the professor. "Although so much is not plainly expressed, I believe that he was the reckless murderer of his innocent wife and child."

"He is a mad fool," replied the professor, "to whom I do not give credit for enough courage to perform such an act. On this point he never speaks plainly; and the question is, whether it be not a mere fancy that he took any part in the death of his wife and child. He now returns to painting marble; and this very night he will finish the altar. This puts him in a good-humour, and you may learn something about this critical affair from his own mouth."

I must confess that the thought of passing midnight in the church alone with Berthold made me shudder a little, now I had read his history. I thought that there might be a little of the devil in him in spite of his good-humour and frank deportment; and I chose rather to be in his company that very noon in the clear sunlight.

I found him upon the scaffold, reserved and in an ill-humour, painting the veins of marble. Climbing up to him, I reached him the pots, while he stared at me with amazement. "I am your helpmate," said I softly, and this drew a smile from him. Now I began to talk of his life, so as to let him know that I was acquainted with all; and he seemed to believe that he himself had, on that night, communicated every thing. Very, very gently I came to the frightful catastrophe, and then said suddenly--"Did you actually, in your unholy madness, murder your wife and child?"

At this he let the paint-pot and the pencil fall; and, staring at me with a hideous countenance, as he raised both his hands, cried out, "No, these hands are unstained by the

43

blood of my wife--of my son! Another such word and I will dash myself down from the scaffolding with you, so that both our heads shall be shattered on the stone floor of the church."

At this moment I felt my situation rather odd, and deemed it advisable to change the subject. "Look here, dear Berthold," said I, as quietly and coolly as possible; "see how that ugly dark yellow is running on the wall."

He turned his eyes to the spot, and while he painted out the yellow, I slipped gently down the scaffold, left the church, and went to the professor, to have a hearty laugh at my well-chastised presumption.

My vehicle was repaired, and I left G----, after Professor Aloysius Walter had solemnly promised that in case any thing happened to Berthold, he would communicate it in writing immediately.

About half a year elapsed, when I actually received a letter from the professor. He expressed himself in very prolix terms of praise about our meeting at G----, and wrote as follows about Berthold:--"Soon after your departure affairs took a singular turn with our whimsical painter. He became suddenly quite cheerful, and finished, in the most splendid style, the great altar-piece, which is now the wonder of every body. He then vanished; and, as he took nothing with him, and a few days afterwards we found a hat and stick lying near the O---- stream, we are all of opinion that he met a voluntary death."

J. O.

[1] These "Fantasie-Stuecke" are a collection of tales, &c., by Hoffmann, and purport to be leaves from the journal of a travelling enthusiast. J. O.

[The end]

www.ingramcontent.com/pod-product-compliance
Lightning Source LLC
Chambersburg PA
CBHW030543180626
46810CB00005B/1987